12,380

Brook, Judy
   Tim Mouse visits the farm.   N.Y., Lothrop,
Lee & Shepard, 1977.
   unp.   illus.(pt.col.)

   I.Title.

TIM MOUSE
VISITS THE FARM

For my friends
the Bartletts
who used to live at
Barleybeans Farm

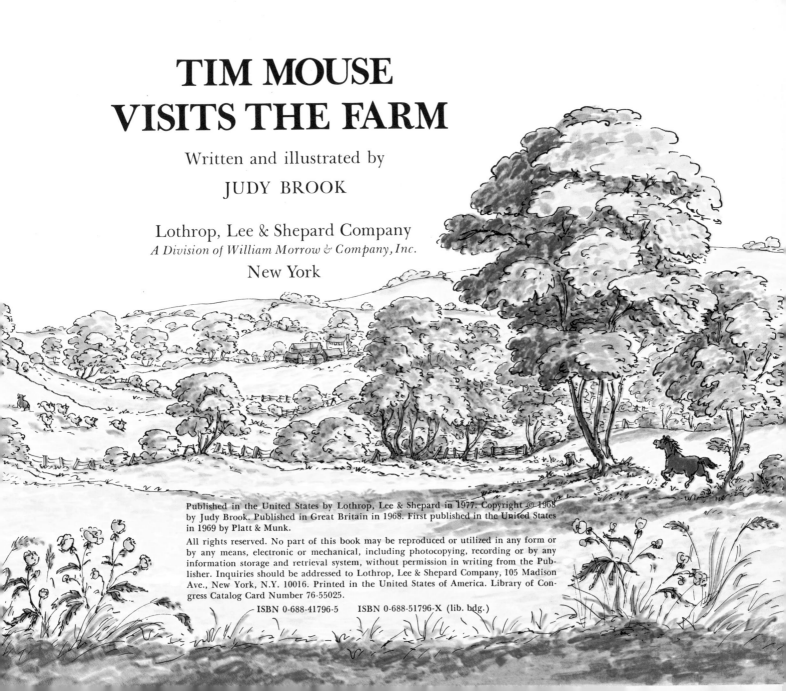

TIM MOUSE VISITS THE FARM

Written and illustrated by

JUDY BROOK

Lothrop, Lee & Shepard Company
A Division of William Morrow & Company, Inc.

New York

Published in the United States by Lothrop, Lee & Shepard in 1977. Copyright © 1968 by Judy Brook. Published in Great Britain in 1968. First published in the United States in 1969 by Platt & Munk.

ISBN 0-688-41796-5   ISBN 0-688-51796-X (lib. bdg.)

One hot sunny afternoon, Tim Mouse was
strolling over the fields when he met
Mr. Brown carrying a little milk pail.
"Oh Tim," said Mr. Brown, "do you know
where I can find a nice cool drink of milk?"
"Yes, of course," said Tim. "The only place is
Barleybeans Farm where six cows live. Come on."
And off they set for the farm.

When they arrived, it was all most beautifully peaceful and quiet.

Milking was over, and the cows were dozing lazily in the yard.

Mr. Brown and Tim looked nervously all around them for cats and dogs,

but none were to be seen.

"Let's go this way," said Tim. "We must find the dairy." And he led the way,

through the granary and stable, past old Punch the cart horse, snoozing peacefully, and out into the yard again. But they still couldn't see the dairy. Mr. Brown began to feel terribly agitated.

Tim, however, became extremely bold, it was all so quiet and peaceful.
Without even consulting Mr. Brown, he set off across the yard,
past the sleeping geese

and some hens taking a dust bath. Poor Mr. Brown followed, expecting
something to pounce on them at any moment.

Around the old cart went Tim, and right in front of fat old Flossie with
her babies, snoring loudly on a pile of dirt.

"Oh Tim, please, my nerves—please go slower," begged Mr. Brown.

But Tim only hurried on faster and faster, right across the middle of the
yard, under the very noses of the enormous sleeping cows!

Poor Mr. Brown was so frightened, he followed Tim feeling more like a
jelly than a hedgehog.

But on went Tim, under a fence, around by the duck pond

under another fence, and all the way up the vegetable garden path.

By now Mr. Brown was quite speechless with fright, expecting cats and dogs
to leap out of the cabbages at any moment!

Then, suddenly, Tim stopped. They had come straight into the flower garden.

There in front of them was a ginger cat, curled up asleep on a table, and sprawled out in front of the back door

were two dogs, Tip the collie and old Blackie!

Mr. Brown and Tim rushed through the first door they could see, and actually found themselves in the dairy at last.

But to their dismay
all the milk was in
enormous cans, and
quite impossible to reach.
Mr. Brown was ready to
cry with disappointment.
But Tim went straight
out into the yard, to
ask a cow for some milk.

He walked boldly over to
a cow called Buttercup,
put his paws in his mouth,
and whistled!
"Oooooh a mouse!"
mooed Buttercup, leaping up.
"Oooooh a mouse a mouse!"
mooed all the cows,
jumping up together.
And the next moment,

the whole yard went mad! Jumping, bucking, kicking, flapping. Such a
commotion of bounding cows, squealing pigs and frantic birds, Barleybeans
Farm had never seen!

"Oooooh a mouse a mouse a mouse," mooed the silly cows, as Tim and Mr. Brown
made a wild dash for safety, through hysterical pigs and chickens.

"Oh dear oh dear a mouse a mouse," mooed Buttercup, and she leaped—

over the fence, causing panic to the ducks, over the next fence, right
across the vegetables, with the other cows following. They knocked down
the runner beans, ruined the carrots and trampled on the cabbages

as they galloped on and on.

Right across the flower beds, wrecking all the flowers, over the lawn,

out of the gate, and down the lane.

"Ooooh a mouse, a mouse," mooed the silly cows.
"Buttercup, Daisy, Rose, Sally, Poppy, Polly,
come home," shouted poor John the farmer.
But the cows galloped on and on.
Down the lane,

over some fences, right across the
cricket field, and through the village.

"Buttercup, Daisy, Rose, Sally, Poppy, Polly, *go home*,"
barked all the dogs.
"Oooooh a mouse, a mouse, go home yourselves,"
mooed the silly cows, galloping faster and faster.
Right through the village,

down some more lanes, over fences and ditches, then away
over the hills and meadows, for miles and miles—

and miles.

The sun went down, the dew began to fall, and all around the countryside
the hills and valleys echoed with poor John the farmer calling,

"Buttercup, Daisy, Rose, Sally, Poppy, Polly, please oh please come home,"

until the very middle of the night. Then at last he brought them home, quite exhausted. And no one ever knew it was only one small mouse called Tim who had caused such a terrible commotion!

Now all this time, while John the farmer was trying to get his cows home,
back at Barleybeans farm everybody had calmed down again.
Then Mr. Brown and Tim decided it was time to go home. They peeped out from
their hiding place, but there was the cat, prowling up and down, fortunately
on the other side of the yard. Mr. Brown and Tim waited until she at last
slunk off around the house. Then they ran over to the stable,

past old Punch again, through the granary, as fast as their legs would go. And they didn't stop running until they reached the safety of the fields.

Then they walked sadly home to Tim's house. In the distance they could hear "Buttercup, Daisy, Rose, Sally, Poppy, Polly, please oh please come home."

"Oh dear," said Tim, "poor Mr. Farmer. How silly cows are! I'm sorry, Mr. Brown."

"It wasn't your fault," said Mr. Brown. "Cows are just silly, that's all."

When they arrived home, they sat silent and miserable for a long time.
Then Tim had an idea. He slipped outside without telling Mr. Brown
and left the little milk pail by the door, with a note. The note said,
"½ a pint of milk today, please!"

And the next morning—there was the milk pail FULL OF MILK!

"Tim, Tim, Tim, quick quick, come and look!" shouted Mr. Brown, dancing up and down with excitement.

"*Hooooray* hooooray hoooeee," squeaked Tim, leaping about like a grasshopper. Then they joined paws and danced and danced,

and danced.

Round and round, up and down, leaping and prancing over the fields,
laughing, whooping, and singing the wonderful news to everyone.

Who could the milkman be? They never discovered. But from that day to this,
if Mr. Brown leaves a note outside, the milk arrives like magic, every morning,
and they have never tried to ask the silly cows again.